Eloise Visits the Zoo

KAY THOMPSON'S ELOISE

Eloise Visits the Zoo

STORY BY **Lisa McClatchy**

ILLUSTRATED BY **Tammie Lyon**

Ready-to-Read

Simon Spotlight
New York   London   Toronto   Sydney   New Delhi

SIMON SPOTLIGHT

An imprint of Simon & Schuster Children's Publishing Division

1230 Avenue of the Americas

New York, NY 10020

First Simon Spotlight hardcover edition September 2018

First Aladdin Paperbacks edition May 2009

Copyright © 2009 by the Estate of Kay Thompson

All rights reserved, including the right of reproduction

in whole or in part in any form.

"Eloise" and related marks are trademarks of the Estate of Kay Thompson.

SIMON SPOTLIGHT, READY-TO-READ, and colophon are

registered trademarks of Simon & Schuster, Inc.

For information about special discounts for bulk purchases, please contact Simon & Schuster

Special Sales at 1-866-506-1949 or business@simonandschuster.com.

The text of this book was set in Century Old Style.

Manufactured in the United States of America 0818 LAK

2 4 6 8 10 9 7 5 3 1

Library of Congress Control Number 2009004057

ISBN 978-1-5344-2039-7 (hc)

ISBN 978-1-4169-8642-3 (pbk)

My name is Eloise.
I am a city child.

I am also an animal lover.
I love Weenie, my dog.

I love Skipperdee, my turtle.

And I love, love, love
going to the zoo!

"It is summertime!"
I say to Nanny.

The perfect time
for going to the zoo.

Nanny and I wear
our safari best.

We wear our safari hats.
And our safari vests.

And, of course, we bring
our safari camera
and our binoculars.

There is so much
to see at the zoo!

"To Africa first, Nanny," I say.
Nanny and I study the
lowland gorillas.

We say hello back
to the lions.

The giraffe tries
to lick my hand.
"No, no, no, Eloise!"
says Nanny.

Oh, I love, love, love
giraffes!

"To Australia now, Nanny,"
I say.
Nanny and I take pictures
of the kangaroos.

We sketch the koalas in their eucalyptus trees.

"Here, Nanny," I say.
"Would you like to
   feed the lorries too?"

"No, no, no, Eloise!"
says Nanny.

Oh, I love,
love, love
lorries.

"To North America!"
I yell to Nanny.
We howl along with
the gray wolves.

We search for the black bear.

We visit the petting zoo. "May I take a billy goat home, Nanny?" I ask.

"No, no, no, Eloise!"
Nanny says.
Oh, I love, love, love
billy goats.

"To the nursery last,"
I say to Nanny.
We sing to the baby
chimpanzee.

We whisper hello to
the sleeping wombat.

A volunteer asks Nanny if we would like to see the new baby elephant.

"Oh, yes!" Nanny and
I say together.

Oh, I love, love, love
the zoo!